THE BEAUTIFUL /
/ PALACE PRAYERS
-POEMS & PROSE-

Nefisa UK
Washington DC – San Diego

The Beautiful / Palace Prayers

05. Food not prepared with love, eating out, running away to find home.

Published by Nefisa UK
NEFI-BK06
First Edition

ISBN 10:   0-9555024-5-4
ISBN 13:   978-0-9555024-5-3

Dissolution Is The Whole Show

When Yusuf invited me to contribute a foreword to 'The Beautiful,' I was at first surprised. Although I enjoy reading poetry, my education in literature is wanting, and my tastes run to work that most "serious" critics and scholars deem pedestrian. Who am I to comment on this young artist's latest collection? With characteristic enthusiasm, however, Yusuf's invitation quelled my self-doubt, insisting that 'The Beautiful' is made up of poems "for normal people who do not normally read poetry." Well, in that case, it is a privilege and a joy for *this* normal person to introduce a collection of poems, verse, and prose written "for normal people"!

> They are a good species.
> Clean and caring;
> Made mostly of water and forgiveness

> - The Beautiful

Normal people are very much in need of poetry, and perhaps especially so today, when the art is generally neglected. Words are powerful entities, every one an invocation, yet we too often use them carelessly. Poetry, like prayer, can serve as a corrective, reminding us that words conjure meaning and that they have a felt, physical component. As critic and philosopher George Steiner writes, "the meanings of poetry and the music of those meanings... are also of the human body." Appropriately, Yusuf refers to the italicized and apparently random words that he includes in some of his poems as 'body echoes.' "*Carbunkle. Crellis. / Pulse-if. peaces.*" or "*Que Que*" are not intelligible formulations but, when read aloud, they aren't exactly jibberish either. They supply somatic meaning, as do the poems' rhythms. Yusuf's strongest poetry or verse has a perceptible pulse; in some cases, I notice my head slowly bobbing as I read. This is not insignificant. Beat and rhythm are primal properties, manifestations of the infinite, unfathomable being within which we reside and of which we are composed.

> Echoes
> of the original
> Voice
> From the original
> Breath

> - Ramadhan 26

Ludwig Wittgenstein insisted that earnest philosophers should "descend into primeval chaos and feel at home there" if they expect to produce worthy work. I extend the same requisite to artists. Yusuf draws pictures, makes films, and writes poems, novels, and songs, but he is, above all, a mystic. And mysticism, in its quest to directly experience elemental truths, necessitates Wittgenstein's appreciation of the primeval and the chaotic; ancient disorder is at the root of everything. In most cases, the mystical perspective is merely an uncommon one; mystics survey and respond to the same earthly, material realm that the rest of us do. But they disregard accepted classifications and train themselves to mindfully observe and reinterpret their surroundings, locating the extraordinary in the mundane. As Henry David Thoreau, a 19th century mystic, lamented, "All this [splendor] is perfectly distinct to an observant eye and yet could easily pass unnoticed by most." Mystics reawaken their capacity for reflective wonder and, in doing so, experience a kind of rebirth into a vaster dimension of human experience.

So reborn into sublime beauty, mystics strive toward the transcendent. Both Wittgenstein and Thoreau can be described as transcendentalists; Yusuf qualifies, too. Like the two philosophers, he finds in his observations of the world cause for a fundamental optimism. Unlike them, his writing is generally informal and devoid of pretension. His poems give readers the impression of a devout Sufi Muslim happy at play in our waking, sensual dream. In the collection's title poem, Yusuf writes "Awake in this dream / Where abstract clouds calmly keep us. / Where birds secretly make love in public and / Give voice to the current of joy which / Slices through us in a day." Again, in 'Back Amongst Men (Drowned),' he references this dreamed life: "Or as I have also interpreted it / .God is a laughing dream." No doubt, the poems' author, laughing, singing, eyes wide and sparkling, would appear mad to many of his fellows. This is to their discredit. They have forgotten (or failed to learn) how to look. Mystics, like many philosophers and artists, are too easily dismissed as lunatic or eccentric. Yusuf's ability to see through the veil of our cultural forgetfulness informs his aesthetic imagination and invigorates his art.

> Silk veils, dark and weightless
> Are being removed from her countenance
> Time after Time
> Each day I ready myself to know her better
> Each day, closer

> - Wahad

But not all that Yusuf observes is felicitous. The most biting poem included, 'Ramadhan 23: Only To Be With You And No-one Else,' is a reaction against the politicization of Islam and a celebration of his intimate relationship with Allah. After rejecting the "bloody bridge builders / Shmoozers or politicians" and others who "come to the Mosque smiling in your suit," Yusuf writes, "I wish to be alone / And serious / And deeper in love / With the only one who ever matters." The striking seriousness of his personal communion with G-d is important; discipline is one of the central currents running through the poems included in 'The Beautiful.' In 'Waiting (A Song for Guitar),' Yusuf writes, "I *do* believe in magic but first you gotta work at it." Hope and love, he reminds readers, are nurtured through dedicated ritual and practice.

A visual artist, I appreciate the centrality of discipline in a life committed to aesthetics. Like Yusuf, though, I am also mystically inclined. Paintings, sculptures, and other hand-crafted objects are among my adored icons but, if I work at it, I can find occasion for worship in every place, in every form, in every moment. The European starling that paraded on the sidewalk in front of me this morning warranted exaltation. In his iridescent dream coat and brilliant yellow bill, I see cause for startling, smiling celebration. For some other pedestrians, the bird, a representative of a despised species, may be ignorable or irrelevant. For others, my viewing the starling as a manifestation of the Divine amounts to idolatry. So, too, might the dirty, discolored Queens sidewalk be deemed a cement calf by unimaginative or close-minded "believers." Yet, striding on such a sidewalk today, my thoughts range through eons of geologic time to consider the ancient rock and mud, precursors to and components of the concrete that I now tread upon, from which our kind eventually emerged on crude limbs as a gasping, fish-reptile thing.

The salt-pepper sugar mills on this table look like planets.
I want to know the word for planet in as many different languages as
possible.

- Celestial

Doubtless some of those who consider themselves religious don't share my enthusiasm for our scaled, long-snouted ancestors. But I'm not concerned with narrow definitions of religion. I believe that humility, wonder, gratitude, and communion are the four pillars of genuine religious practice, and the mental stretching engendered by the work of scientists, philosophers, and artists is an integral part of any intellectually rigorous, honest religious life. And, love, too, is a bit like religion. The same four pillars are fundamental to it. As Douglas Thorpe writes, "[love] demands of us a new way of being in our old world." Religious mysticism is a love affair with The All. It's not always easy, but religious attunement can turn each day, each hour, or each instant, into "a new way of being." Reading Yusuf's poetry, I'm reminded that every step is a psalm, every directed gaze is a prayer.

I'm also reminded that we both enjoy watching starlings.

Christopher Reiger, May 1, 2010
Queens, New York City

THE BEAUTIFUL

&

PALACE PRAYERS

THE BEAUTIFUL

Look! At all of these people.
They are full of sweet beauty!
None of them know
As they glide on autopilot
Which is another way to say
Live with instinct, soulfully

As these years, fives and decades fall off our shoulders
And our belly's expand and
Knowledge deepens

Movements turn us and
Tumult teaches us to keep
Rising, swerving and coasting

Glittering across like the
Pacific
Priceless on a sunset
                    soundless.

Awake in this dream
Where abstract clouds calmly keep us.
Where birds secretly make love in the public and
Give voice to the current of joy which
Slices through us in a day.

Dot-Dot-Purple and Palaces
Says the starling in approximate translation.
Star-Star-Chandeliers and
Bread on the wind-ind-ind.

Awake in this dream of slow cars in the city,
Shaking cups of Polystyrene

Filled with pieces of silvered human-ness
Transacted endlessly until they find their one true home.

In finding their way, they are touched by the trembling
Unsure digits
The tools of a tree-like people who speak
One true language

And yet constantly act as if they cannot understand
one another,
Cannot read eyes or intentions
And need translators with turtle-tongues.

They are a good species.

Clean and caring;
Made mostly of water and forgiveness.

Only a very small portion of them truly swim in flames.

The rest are badly disguised dancers.

18th May 2009, 17th & L St. Washington DC

THE FIRST

Que Que

Over your gravestone I am still
Attracted. To you.
Or is it the life that you were filled with?
The strange jewels you kept inside
On loan, or a part of you
Who were also on loan
Paying a rent
For your days of reflection and skincrystal and
Glowing
         mud
Luminescent as your traces of personality.

You chewed gum sometimes
You did other Earthly things too
But without talking
Without signing, so that one day
I could lay in the strange sun
Sitting on a steel chair
And think about you

Wondering if you ever really existed
Trying to remember how it felt
When we held each other
In that perfect shape

A DAY OF EXISTENCE

The voice volvic revolving and vaping for fine
Air of distinction.
The feel thunder of frog-chorus and black stars
Sperm spawn in the
Sky of Eye
The cut crater of care and unkindness in a stolen me-self.
The egg-wonder of a round Earth
Newborn to a child of daydreams

God, give me a cradle and
Rock my head back to the timeless
Sleep rhythm of newborn
Before world wide recognition
When any moment at all
Was okay to fall asleep into

Far off in the macrocosm of me and you
Where fibres, strands and tambourines
Dream of a rhythm which
Once manifested into being
Would curl and bind all blood
Back to the born beginning

Blind ocean wavers softly
Covered in snow
Moving across miles of beyond
Frontiers
Melting and tumbling
Breathing and billowing

Carbunkle . Crellis .
  Pulse-if . peaces .

Sun find its way to soul
Birds bring along belief
  By way of wings and
      Precise, clean movement

No jitters but for the fear of
Peace
      It's face shining down on my lungs
                    inside
From some heated   chamber
                inner

Chambre
Shombliss
Shell
Shine

It is dramatic
The automatic sky
Is like the sea to
An expanding eye

THE AUTOMATIC SKY

On perfect Spring mornings
God puts a clear blue sky in our pockets
Pats us a few times and says
"On your way!"

THE MERCIFUL CHEERFUL

Alfalfa Fortune
Yeast Destiny

Clouds Disperse
A field of Wheaten
Gold for a Sun of God
And skittering seedlings
Rushing in for lunch
To a Mother Magnanimous

THE MIRACLE MAKER

UNDEAD (SURVIVOR)

Bursting elements of despair
Salt-filling lung sacks
Desperate for air

God is almighty is this
Borderless Ocean.
God is the Powerful
Perennial Planetary
God is my God is my
Punisher
        Plunger

You are my Master
My Mercy
        Disaster

My mover
My drama
My final of words

                                    My father
                                    My father
                            My giver of Earth

BACK AMONGST MEN (DROWNED)

There is mineral all surrounding me
Huge capacities

Mark-in points are on people's faces
As if they know precisely when they
Want to begin

There are conscious leaves all surrounding me
Too-wittering
Sensical logic runs through the
Regular poets' poems
As if even they are incapable of paying anything but
Lip service to the quaint notion of 'mystery'

.Alif Lam Meem.
        Or as I have also interpreted it
.God is a laughing dream.

They Talk / So Do He

For Ishmael Butler

No guardian guides you
Through the impassioned world of
Repeats and highlights
No nobility nexus
Noble nebulae
Are dreams

Know your place
Hunch your back
Scrunch your face

☯

He Believes in You
He waits for You
Through the repeat doublesin
The over exposure and the
Animality.

He reforms a blown dandelion
Down from all your disparate dredges
To your dreams - levitation

HIP-HOP VERSE WRITTEN TO STREET DRUMS
Thanks to the protesting Workers Unions of Washington DC

Open up the morning let the sun shine
Ma God put in certain people the power to rhyme
Ma Lord Will what he will when he wield time
M'Allah's movements and touches make a man shine
Even in his prime 'n if he king of the hill
Ma Maker mark a miscarriage [on u] 'n he make you spill
Spill out your guts or cholera he could make you ill
Kill all your water
Dried essence an'
Hide your presence
So you a shadow of your former without his blessings
Some typa Richard Nixon lesson
Or Nebuchadnezzar message
For the blessed beings *being* all over this damn *dunya*[1]
Deemed worthy to flex-swerve
An' live life curvy and round
Your journey's pebbles on the ground
You yearn-y for straight lines _____
But it's .dot. .dot. #pound#
And ?Question? mark
This [early] life is a Merciful Arc
It make a dart from the light to the dusty dark
And in between it there's art
And in between it there's heart
The beats (go) beauty-full to the end (the start)

---

[1] Islamic term for this world; emphatically, its material aspect.

13

WAITING (A SONG FOR GUITAR)

[sing in all the spaces, "I'm waaaiting"]

...

For a slow computer, should be doing its duty

...

For some grace-light sun to come shining through me

...

For Jalal-ud-Din Rumi
But the Prophet Muhammad first

Gimme a vision inna dream and I'll sing it in a verse

Waiting for the gold dust, see how it control us

Waiting for the inspiration, Allah on the late bus

For the floating thoughts in my mind, become solid!

Gaseous focus, procrastinator-*malik*[2]

Cellulite, soft, indiscipline addict

For my mind and heart t'get involved and active

I *do* believe in magic but first you gotta work at it

Everywhere I look I see distraction pockets
Everywhere I think I see distraction pockets
Devils in the daytime, dumbing me down
Pebbles to the devils who be runnin' me down

---

[2] Arabic for 'king'

{Be a} rebel to the devils and snatch back your crown
Your face is so beautiful when your heart is round
Sound, sonorous, sing softly through your sad eyes
This life is a struggle I see so many sad eyes
We just want somebody to tell us it's alright
To put their hand on our soul, w'some assertive control
W'some deep depth below and a smile that grow slow
But you got more forgiveness in your heart than you can
Know
Don't you think it's time you took it easy and slow?
Don't you think it's 'bout that time for encouragement?
Be lovely to yourself and the whole world'll follow.

CELESTIAL

The salt-pepper sugar mills on this table look like planets.
I want to know the word for planet in as many different languages as
possible.

I am a planetary man
With atmospheres and clouds within

Through my kindness and generosity of spirit
I support life.
.All praise is for God.

Unattended, I grow wild, unruly
Pressured and interfered with, I withdraw into silence
Tucking down the forming lava

My continents are moving, imperceptible
Converge-Diverge
So that today I might love discipline
And tomorrow I might go back to wilderness
Sweet delicious, freeing chaos

When I sleep I see stars

When I dawn, a lulling majesty

                              oncoming

WAHAD

There is an unknown beautiful woman
To whom I have pledged my life

Her face is: I can't see.
It floats in the sky of thoughts
The open sky of maybe

Silk veils, dark and weightless
Are being removed from her countenance
Time after Time

Each day I ready myself to know her better
Each day, closer

God make me small in my own eyes and
Large in the eyes of others.

Make me as clean and precise as a sparrow

Sparrows do not think much of themselves
-Too busy-
Yet anyone who notices them, truly sees them
Cannot but help to admire them
Can find no fault in their character
In their nature.

The people are obtuse when you are
Cruel when you are
When high, you see them as poor creatures in need of
attention and love.
Nothing but attention and love to
                          bring them around

When you cannot impress yourself anymore
When you are a stagnant repeat
Nothing becomes as tempting as the idea of
Leaving everything
                  where it stands
                      and
Running off to the mountains for some
Ice-Pak Inner-Peace ™

No flight is more valuable than being able to sit somewhere
local and stare for an hour, nothing but sun and wind.

Nothing but patience, which sires peace.

18

Eyelids are sunglasses
So, once again
. close them .

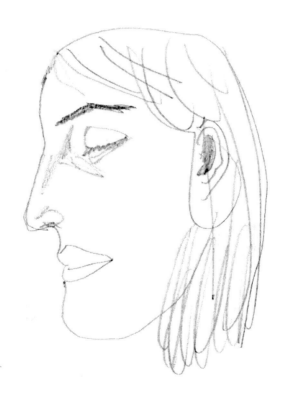

THE BIRD (SPARROW)

To *chirrip* and *chu* or *chee*
To spin or dance with energy
To create a Cairo
A New York
A Mercutian destiny so great as to need to
Implode with the force of its own weight

I won't weight
I'll make it before my fingers fall off
I won't stay(le)
I'll leave my mama's house
And shine myself up again

Rubbed and refined against a whole new thang
Walk the new streets spit the brand new slang
Dogs smell no fear in this heart that I own
Birds come and see me through the windows of home
Conversate in thought-hills, tiles and trills
{We} speak the language responsible for spinely chills
What it kills is the presence in pride and politics
From which I build bricks, make a whole new home
The Palace of Positives with the Cloudy Dome
And the jets that's Minarets yet formed in Stone
Aim t'ward the sphere in the Springtime Zone

Flirt with the moon, dreaming of later
Alone with my Lord deep inner-the-crater
Shaded cave, blue & gold candles
Glow in the gloom-gleam-gladness, forgiveness
Sing, keep singing, be the Sufi stalwart
Stubborn, even stiff when it comes to your freedom
Steadfast today, 'cos you wanna be the Sea

Sacrifice now, if you wanna be the bird
Deep in silence, where you find the word

KUJAH?

If it is true, then
That little is sacred, and little pure,

If it is true, then
That people do things behind your back
In a pleasure of shadow and silence

If it is true that as much as they praise you
They can equally revile you
And be disgusted with you

(And it is. For we have done.)

If so
Then where for purity?
Where for things which cannot be opposed?
Where for something true, deeply
Some dignified wood which will never turn
Staying true to its lines of history
Some subtle mountain, tiny and sturdy
Unmovable peg to the dissatisfied
Life of selfishness and greed and
Accepted dissatisfaction

Something to humble the arrogant king we have all become

Who thinks he can get whatever he wants

Deserves what he wants

And is never full

23

JACOBSEN
Translated from Norwegian

"Hone it gracefully," he said, moving his hands across the golden surface as if he were doing Tai-Chi. The young students in the class were all paying respectful attention. After all, this artisan, Brancussi, had been gilding frames and furniture for over 20 years. They were a rag-tag bunch of kids doing their MFA's in fine arts. Most of them were in their mid-20's, and two of them were 40-somethings. The 40-somethings had an on again, off again relationship, man and woman. They were complicated in ways which the younger ones could not understand.

I was also amongst the younger ones. My name is Jacobsen. My friends call me Jacobsen. I have blonde hair, and glasses. I wear a delicious little curling smile on my face at all times, even when I am concentrating or straining myself. It's not necessarily because I feel full of joy all of the day (although I am usually very happily disposed) but rather it's a habit. I got it from my father, Erland. Erland is a fisherman. He sat me down one day, when I was about 8, and he told me this:

"Don't let anybody fool you. If you ever feel that someone is trying to pull the wool over your eyes, call them out straight away, challenge them! Don't worry if you turn out to be wrong, the important thing is that you remain on your toes and alert at all possible times. This world is full of crooks, son. Everyone's trying to get away with whatever they can without being called on it. Don't let them. If you follow this advice, you'll be one of a very select few group of people on this Earth who carry out this work. And it is good work, son. Even if it makes you unpopular, it's work that needs to be done."

Over the years the glass of my mind reflected, refracted and interacted with this single piece of advice in many different ways. Despite the fact that Erland gave advice very freely, and quite often, it was that particular lesson which seemed to run the deepest for him. That was the most repeated, and the one he delivered with most passion: that the world consisted of dishonest people who would try their hardest to get away with not being totally sincere.

When I was 19, and going out a lot at nights, I used to frequent the music clubs in my town. My town was not altogether unfashionable, and certainly had its share of young and aspiring musicians. They all liked to play their guitars and dress up. I knew something about good music too, I thought, and so when I saw music that I didn't like, I would boo. I would always be the only one to do it and most of my friends would be embarrassed (although eventually they laughed if they were sufficiently drunkards). I felt as though the bands shouldn't be allowed to get away with it. Those rotten liars. They surely knew how bad they were, but everyone in the audience was far too polite to do a thing but clap meekly. 'Hypocrites!' I thought. And I booed extra loud until they walked away from the stage. I later told my father what I had done, and why, and he nodded silently, with his eyes closed, like a responsible teacher. "Well done, son," he would say, "it's the only way they'll learn. It's the only way we can make this world more honest and true." I can't say I felt good, inasmuch as being the 'bad guy' ever makes one feel good. Nonetheless, I took some comfort in his approval in those times.

But when I was 21 and in love for the first time, his advice not only became wrong, but dangerous. I rebelled against it whenever it occurred to me, and made a point out of trying to prove him wrong by trusting people who I had no right trusting: total strangers. I left my bags by my seat in the library whenever I needed to get up and urinate, and I asked the least trustworthy-looking person if he could watch over them (usually it was some fat-looking man with a dark beard and a reddish face, someone who looked as dark as the night). To my deepest surprise (which soon became smug affirmation), I never once got robbed, never had my confidence betrayed. It was not even real *confidence*, but more of a theory in practice, a feeling enacted. I held that Erland's views were distorted and wholly incorrect.

After Torrun, who was the first, there were a few other girls. All three of them were from Norway, except the one who was from Sweden. Did I love them as much as my first, Torrun? No way! Not by the hairs on my chin! But I did care for them? Oh yes. Yes I did, deeply. And when my father met them all, he would smile, always in his brown sweater, putting his fork down out of respect, and smiling at them, from the other side of our old oak dinner table. He was grinning because they were young and pretty. This was partly why I was with them. But when we broke up, after some time passed, we would eventually become friends. I loved becoming friends!

I am one of those jolly bastards, always cheerful. It's not easy to hate me. In fact, I'd go so far as to say it's impossible. I'm not being an arrogant one, you understand, it's just that I'm a very simple, cheerful man. Perhaps my booing of the musical bands gave you an impression of me as edgy or cocky, but not in the least! I was just a young boy experimenting then. If you hated me, there'd have to be something wrong with you. It would be like hating a bird. Not birds in general, but one particular bird. That sort of hatred just isn't logical!

There came a time, just before I left Norway to do my MFA in London, that I met a girl. She was unlike any of the others

I had met. Why? I'd like to tell you. For a start, she wasn't all that pretty. Not ugly, of course, but certainly not a head-turner like the rest of the women I'd been with. Secondly she was verging on being portly. Yes, a real handful! Thirdly, (and I'll say something serious here so you don't think me a total sensualist) she was not razor sharp. So, you might ask, why is Jacobsen with a woman who's not a stunner, who's a little round, and is not the sharpest of people? Well, I'd like to tell you. If you are a very rich child, and your parents provide you with a whole room filled to the brim with the latest toys and games to play with, there will come a time, eventually, that you'll want to go outside and look at strange trees and moss. That's natural.

Her name was Rekka. She was an editor at the city paper, she had a very large professional capacity and capability. I didn't admire her for that though. Let me tell you what I liked: she was one of the first girls I had met who seemed to be totally happy with herself. Perhaps I was finally maturing at 24, but after I discovered this about her, I was drawn! Drawn in! Just like a horny young sailor to a pretty young thing standing on the shore. But it wasn't the usual sensuality, of course. It was interest from my, yes I will say it, my heart! And all I could think about was to talk with her, again and again. We always had such great conversations when we spoke. She was so easy to get along with. Perhaps it was because she didn't expect much. I felt no pressure when I was around her. I could be myself, right from the start. It's like a cardboard box which you play with as a child. It's not shiny and expensive, but it's wide open to anything and everything that a lively child can do. A 24 year old is still a very lively child.

I left for University, anyway, and we agreed to stay in touch. What a strange thing to be in touch with someone and not knowing the reason why you keep on writing. We were not 'together,' nor had we yet kissed or even held hands. We had just spoken, met and spoken. And with such affection, yes, with such affection, did I write to Rekka. She wrote back and told me that she was a practitioner of the ancient Chinese art of Tai-Chi. It made me even more intrigued. She told me that she practiced in a park in the Hellerud every Saturday. The fact that she lived in Hellerud was enough to endear her to me. It made me terribly excited to see her again. What was happening to young Jacobsen? I'd like to tell you. I will do so with the words of Prince Rogers Nelson:

There comes a road in every man's journey
A road that he's afraid 2 walk on his own
I'm here 2 tell U that I'm at that road
And I'd rather walk it with U than walk it alone.

This is the song I quoted to her when I wrote to her before the Christmas break. I returned home to Oslo so excited I could barely contain myself on the plane. I was smiling even more so than usual, grinning like a madman! The old man who sat next to me on the plane thought me a special child. Jacobsen was one happy son of a pessimist!

And what a whirlwind holiday it was. I had three weeks, and I intended to make the most of them. We went out for a walk to the park, and I had found myself suddenly stricken with shyness. Something which I had never suffered before. I was so shy in front of her that I could barely ask her to hold hands. That's how bad it was! Yes, it could only mean one thing, love. At least love as I knew it. Naturally then, I brought her to my father's house. When we walked in, he did not get up from the kitchen table, did not put his fork down, and did not grin at her from across the old oak table. He merely stared at her, then to me, and then back to her again, thoroughly bemused. I did not want him to say anything embarrassing (and with Erland, one could never be sure) so I was forced to stay on the offensive throughout dinner, asking him question after question about his work, about old friends, people in the neighbourhood etc. He answered my questions with a sly grin, at his own measured, suspicious pace, and in a very deliberate manner, stroking his chin and sizing me up as he did so. He regarded me with narrowed, suspicious eyes, and after answering the fifth question, he tagged on a little ad-lib,

"But all that's neither here nor there, Jacobsen. Why don't you tell me what's *really* going on here?"

"What do you mean Erland?"

"You come back for Christmas, you bring this girl Rekka to our dinner table, and you start acting all shifty!"

Rekka excused herself politely and ran out of the room whimpering slightly. Poor girl! But it was lucky that she did not stay to hear more of my forthright father,

"Why did you do that, Erland?"

"What do you mean? I'm not the one who brings ugly heffers into the house! You could at least have brought a looker back for me, Jacobsen! Come on now! That's unfair of you, don't you think?"

"I LIKE HER, ERLAND! I Think... She might even be the one I want to marry!"

He shooed me away like a fly, waving his hand and blowing some old air out of his resigned lips; unimpressed.

"You do what you like! Just make sure she's not trying to pull the wool over your eyes, son. It would be a real crime if you married a heffer and she also turned out to be a bitch too, if you know what I mean."

I shook my head and sighed at my father, he was damaged goods beyond repair. I told him I would be back later.

Obviously I had to convince Rekka that my father was slightly eccentric, and that he meant no harm. Which was true, in fact, but it felt like a lie when I was saying it. When you are trying to calm a female who is crying, everything you say feels like a lie somehow. Perhaps it's because you are trying so hard! I don't know. Gosh! Life!

The thing about Rekka was, she was very passive. Initially this was something I treasured about her, because it came across as a shy sort of humility. But the more time I spent with her, the more I noticed that she would never give any indication that she wanted you to get closer. Most girls would do this, they'd say certain things in conversations that made it obvious, or do certain things even. It was almost the opposite with her. I would always be the one to call her, to ask her out, to suggest things, just to initiate conversations. And when I looked back I realised that I had also been the one to initiate writing letters. She had never been a very quick responder to the letters I sent from University.

One day, in my last week, she held a party with all of her friends in her apartment. I was impressed, I must say. She had many friends, and they all seemed to like her. She was no secret, her bright personality had won her plenty of admirers and everyone seemed to like her as much as I. At the end of the night, after everyone had gone, I went for a walk with her. Against my better judgment, I kissed her. It was very nice, and she reciprocated silently. I felt as if some ice had been melted. I stayed over there with her, but she told me I had to sleep in the front room. I didn't mind. What a fun adventure it was! Sleeping in someone else's home! I looked up at her different ceiling, so happy at what I had accomplished, so excited about the future, the next morning, and all the unknown things which might unravel from there.

The next morning I woke to find her gone. I was alone in her apartment. She had left me a note by the table. It said this:

I really think we should just be friends. That's what I would like.
Take care, R.

I couldn't quite believe what I read. Such a brief letter! So cold! Well, it was an outrage! 'How could she?' I thought. 'What did I do wrong?' I thought. My first instinct was to call her cellular phone, but I decided against it. The mature side of old Jacobsen kicked in and told me to wait. 'She'll come around,' I thought, 'just give her some time and some space.'

But she never called me again. And as the days wore on, my pride also was worn down. 'What is she doing? Is she prepared to let the whole relationship disappear just like that? *Why?* What happened?' I couldn't come up with any answers. But the more days went by without word from her, the more strongly I decided that I would not call her either. 'Why should I,' I thought, 'When I was the one doing all the calling and chasing all the time?' And the week passed, and the holiday was over, and I was due to return to London. Poor old Jacobsen was miserable. What irreparable wreckage occurs when once stubborn pride has made its presence felt! I spent the last few nights at my father's place.

One night he brought out a bottle of mjød when we sat at the old oak dinner table. The low lamp dangled above us giving yellow light for the winter night. As well as his brown sweater, which he wore every evening, he also smelled of the sea, and of fish. Always. But it wasn't a raw smell. Not like the smell you would smell when he was actually out at sea holding a fish in his hand. It was like the smell of the memory of the sea. The memory of the sea, kept warm in a little place.

I inspected the bottle, which he had passed me.

"I didn't know you drank this sort of stuff, Erland?"
"Oh yes! Only on special occasions, Jacobsen."
"Isn't it a little posh for a simple man like you?"
"Well... Let's just say when you've smelled as much fish guts as I have in my lifetime, you can afford to live well once in a while."

I forced a natural laugh, but it was still far-away. I was still thinking about Rekka.

"Forget the heffer son. You did the right thing letting her go. There are plenty more beauties lying out there in the land just waiting to be plucked up. Get over it."
"That's easier to say than it is to do, Erland."

He took a sip of the mjød, savouring the honeyed taste in his mouth, swirling it around a while and then gulping it loudly. He poured himself a little more and raised his glass ceremoniously up to the ceiling. The dangling lamp bumped and bumbled onto the arm of his brown sweater.

"Here's to that whore of a woman, your mother! My God, she was the best thing I ever had!"

32

And down went another gulp, without the savouring this time.

"Do you think it was easy when she left me, son? I bet you were too young to remember, hm? Too young to notice, I think."
"I remember you crying on the dinner table once."
"Yes, well. I did plenty of that too. It's not easy when a woman gives you no explanation. Even today sometimes I think of it and wonder."
"There's something I didn't tell you, father."
"Hmm? What?"
"Well, I didn't leave Rekka."
"What d'you mean? Yes you did! DON'T YOU LIE TO M..."
"No, father, I was lying... I didn't leave her. She just left me. That was that. She just left and she won't return my calls and she didn't tell me anything!"

Erland took some time to think about it. He burped once, with his mouth closed as always. He was not a very strong drinker. After some time he said this,

"So. Rekka left you just like Anna left me, hm?"
"I suppose so."
"Do you know what options lay before you, Jacobsen? I'd like to tell you. Number one, you can go out, and get yourself another woman, a real pretty one this time too! Or number two, you can end up like me, drinking mjød every Sunday night and doing nothing special with your life. I'd like to tell you, son, just what a woman is. Just what a woman can DO. They give birth to you, first of all, okay so you know all about that, no big secrets there, you're a grown boy now, you know about that. But did you know that each man is born more

33

than once in his life? Hm? NO! You didn't. That's because you haven't really been born yet, son. Not just yet!"

He slapped my thigh when he said the following sentence,

"That's why you have to go and get yourself another woman!"

"I don't want anyone else. I'm so angry."
"Oooooh yes! Oooo-hoooo, I'd like to tell you about anger, son! Remember when our kitchen door broke and we had to go and repair it?"
"Yes."
"Well, it didn't break! You were at school one day, I was sitting here feeling sad and feeling, yes, I'll say it, ANGRY! And you know what I did? I smashed the damned kitchen door myself! Ripped it right from its hinges, I did!"

His eyes were wide, wild and mad, and he ripped a comparatively smaller (invisible) door from its hinges as he spoke.

I thought of the broken kitchen door. And remembered the indelible image of the ripped-out hinges. Even at 9 years-old I remember detecting something slightly odd about the way my father explained it. 'Doors didn't just break on their own,' was the sort of vague feeling I felt back then. And those twisted hinges now looked so violent and mangled in my memory.

"It was the same thing with the shower curtain too. I was having a shower one day, and the anger, it just seized me, son! And I ripped that damned curtain off those rings with all the anger in the world. And what did it get me, hm? What did it get us? A new damned shower curtain! And nothing else!"

"Erland?"

"What?"

"You know how you always say that people can't be trusted, and that they are all trying to pull the wool over your eyes?"

"What about it?"

"Do you think you say that just because mother left us?"

"Well. ... Well, let me put it to you like this Jacobsen, back when I was with your mother, I trusted everyone. I loved everyone too. Sounds funny doesn't it? And now, now I wouldn't trust my best friend to bait my hook."

He took the bottle of mjød, which was still half full, and began to pour the wine directly into his lap, giggling and laughing as he did so. Good old Jacobsen smiled, like a knowing son. I had learned long ago not to stop him when he did such things.

Palace Prayers

RAMADHAN 01

Inner springs gush forth
And rain showers inside of us
Our arable bodies give of themselves
There is no end to what we may saturate
Piscean stars rainbow across the sky of space
From the pitch of birth   to the ink of rebirth
Your mother carved you of Water, God and Greatness
And on you she looks, for confirmation of what she knows.

RAMADHAN 01.1

I will never stop living on local time.
When you are far, I won't mourn you.
My love, it's only local honey that I care for
So do not grieve if you ever find out that which I might never
tell you

That I mourn not your loss when you have been lifted
                Afar and free

RAMADHAN 02

Cherry Coal and Carbon Craters

Half smiles and hidden agendas
Fall away now like a dissolving
Tablet in Water.

We swallow down silence
Everything seems sobered
Suffering is leveled out
As the day is stretched
Across particles of patience

Rolling Pearls dance upon the Strands
The chords twist and fresh fibres are
Created

New angles nullify yesterdays pain-drops

The dawn drops hang with pride off a telephone wire
Twinkling like last nights stars
Telling of today
And the grey truths that will form to manifest

RAMADHAN 03
NO MYSTERY
(A SONG FOR GUITAR)

It's Universal
How I glide
I'm walking
> Circles

That the experienced understand
This thing is patterns, man
N'every symbol interchangeable

But some bright ideas
Can never cyn-ify, pessi-fy
Some shiny things…
Keep you guessing at the taste of a Sip of the Sun

Some soft-sun
Bids you run t'ward it's crux of the Heart-*Haqq*[3]
He's Haqq,
He's *H*everlasting [living] inside

And it's love
He's everlasting, inside
And it's love
It laugh and cry you like the first ride
It's love [x8]

No mystery
Except in the where and the how and hu and the when
But I know what
I just don't really *know* what.

---

[3] 'Truth,' one of the 99 known names of God

RAMADHAN 04
MAY TO DECEMBER
For Dante Terrell Smith

The bells ring around the seasons like happy staircases
The rising bells are all across this horizon of new faces

Your beautiful strangers face dances toward my life
You wear thrilling jewellery the likes of which I've not yet
Seen
Frills of cotton,
Earthed tones with dark silent eyes.
Come to me and shake away the worries of this world with
your sharp
         Snare.
Cut through all the dry truths that I have learnt to believe and
put up with
Slice in half and end the life of that side of me
Who now has the nerve to say, "That's how life is."

Rewind me back to when I was 15
To when I knew just *a little*
Felt just *a little* experienced

But was still wide open enough for an unexpected Love
For a dawn of excitement
Where emotion was mysterious and enchanting
And came to me, seeped in, through some
Inner leak or
Inner well-spring whose whereabouts were silent to me.

Only You.

Rewind me
For a future I can live with.

40

RAMADHAN 05

There is only perfume.
There is only hand-held hearts and
There is always belief, especially in the ignorant.
Systems abound, and yet so many are defensive.
So many systems are defense systems
Aimed at keeping off fear, keeping hunger at bay
Or preserving an already crumbling statue of your ego
Which you try to maintain, pitifully
Without realizing it is long since gone in the eyes of anyone with
insight
And completely insignificant to the rest of the self-obsessed
world
Trying to maintain that statue
You're either going to be ignored
Or seen for what you are.
Best to stop sweating
Stop insisting on your common sense arguments and take a step
out of the lonely oval.

So few.
So few.

RAMADHAN 06
THE MADNESS OF KING JORGE
(UN CHANSON POUR HARMONIUM / ACCORDION)

Il ya bien longtemps
J'étais un enfant
Maintenant, je suis tranquille a nouveau

Je marche sur la plage
Réflexion de mon héritage
Et les visages de mes enfants
Sur les nouvelles pages

J'ai lu trop de livres
J'ai été trop manger
J'ai été trop vouloir
J'ai été tombant de la fenêtre
J'ai besoin d'une tête pour mon couer
J'ai besoin de restriction pour mes doigts
J'ai besoin d'une cloche pour mes mouvements
J'ai besoin d'une chapeau, une écharpe, des gants, et des
lunettes

Et un tapis de priére
Et un cigare sans tabac
Seulement l'air, de la dignité

Et un robe de soie
hahahhaahhahahahhahaa!

Oui, je suis complet
Ici, dans mon palais

RAMADHAN 06
THE MADNESS OF KING JORGE
(A SONG FOR HARMONIUM OR ACCORDION)

Long ago
I was a child
Now, I am calm and new

I walk on the beach
Thinking of my heritage
And the faces of my children
On the new pages

I have read too many books
I have been eating too much
I've been wanting too much
I've been falling from the window
I need a head for my heart
I need a restriction on my fingers
I need a bell for my movements
I need a hat, a scarf, some gloves and sunglasses

And a prayer mat
And a cigarette without tobacco
Just the air of dignity

And a silk dressing gown
hahahhaahhahahahhahaa!

Yes, I am complete
Here in my Palace

RAMADHAN 09

I am a stranger to Calligraphy.
To Arabic.
Arabs who know me well shake their heads
Tell me I don't know what I'm missing
Not being able to comprehend the Qur'an in its original
And I nod earnestly and with
Genuine Sadness, most of the year.

I'm a stranger to these well-intentioned
Pale people all around me.
All of whom I get on so well with
None of whom will get me.
Some want to take bits of me
Add me to their lists
Or screw me
Right down into the world
Straight-jacketed and soiled.

I am a stranger to that black sperm
I used to be.
Whatever drifting *fitrah*[4] there once was
Has been lost in a fog of desires
And dulled, obtuse intentions.

◘

Champagne is fizzed but corked
Fireworks reversed
Candles without flames are thoughts
Seed aimlessly dispersed

---

[4] The Islamic concept of innate, original innocence (or purity, goodness)
present in all of humanity and most keenly felt by children.

Cry, but know that there are no seeds of life in tears
Cry your square heart into a dome of
No rocks, but flowering silk

...Tears *do* have seeds
They are the liquid leaving of your
Earthly needs.

the stained man

RAMADHAN 12
THE VOWS REVOLVE

Awake in a Palace of your heart
Make yourself luminous with water
As a white stallion
Gallops through
Andalusian streams
With refined legs that
Ballerina bend
And a head that holds high
Without pomp
High and yet straight ahead

And when thou walketh thy streets
Keep thine gaze low
Not for the purposes of looking sad
Or thoughtful
But to save life
That which you would otherwise step on
And crush needlessly.

Until thou hath changed the course of thy foot in
 Mid-direction
        and inadvertantly twisted your ankle
   (or almost done so)
 Solely for the sake of avoiding an ant
Until this time
Thou hast not known gentleness.

Understand, thee
That gentleness is what makes the gentleman.
Understand, thee
That tenderness comes not of softness
But of a firmness
And of a discipline

46

Understand that of discipline
-Say, the discipline of prayer-
Comes an enjoyment of that same thing.
Discipline to run breeds a love for running
Discipline to practice ones instrument brings forth
a love for playing it
Discipline to speak good breeds a love of horses
And love of all refined things
Whatever you may find them to be.

Awake in a palace of your own creation.
Awake with a self-made heart
Renewed from your morning vows
Refreshed from your luminous drips

Shahada[5], every morning, *Shahada*

---

[5] Say: *La ilaha ilAllah, Muhamadur-rasul-ulah*

Ramadhan 18

Segovian love tunnels
Seep out into lakes, then oceans.

I am sunbathing in Southern California
By the Pacific
Prehistoric Pacific
All around me are sleepy beautiful people
With small rat-dogs on leashes

     "I could *so* go for an ice-cold Soda
     Or a Champagne with lemon Sorbet!"

Says one of them in her bikini with closed eyes
Under quieting sunglasses.

This, too, is Ramadhan, I think.

I keep my gaze to the Pacific
Palace Pacific

But inevitably my disobedient pupils will sometimes
Drift to the Ocean of woman and her
Effortless beauty
Generous providence
Supple sustenance

That is woman

As smart or soulful as a man can be
He can rarely better her in her sleeping state
Where she breathes calmly
And produces eggs hopefully

She has and always will be hopeful
To endure into middle-age with happiness
She must have faith in male-kind
And be prepared to overlook
All of his crap

Oh woman:

Be a silent preacher
Give a sermon of eyes
A speech of your looks
Have the Machu Picchu in your thoughts
So that when someone looks at you
They will see refined civilisation and
Layered beauty in your eyes
Merely *think* beautiful
And everything else will fall with justice

RAMADHAN 19
THE DARK TRAVELER ON HUMAN DIALOGUE
(A HIP-HOP VERSE)

Cool crud
Sans love
It's a terrible drug
An elegant thug
Strolls down Full-Moon street

Grime and the gravel
And the glass-tips travel
Under foot
That was born
Expecting Amazon juices

This whole world is done in corrugated steel
With serrated edges
And the angles sharp
Cut the clean slice off
Of feelings that want to expand to a smooth top
Sheriff John Brown kills them before they grow
Before they even get a chance to go slow
And live life breathing like the world's on dope
When you feel like the meaning's coming through like smoke
And it spoke through God
With a sneaking feeling
Truth, snaking out the woods and onto your ceiling
Droops, seeping into your cerebral conscious
But still, you don't know correct questions or answers
It's all a magic mush of meshed monosyllabic verbs
It's all a clumsy bang bang bangin' of bad words
And insufficient ears make a mountain of wax turds
Best to just still and pick your nose
Philosophize on something while your nostril hairs grow

But keep a pretty picture in your mental slideshow
So people look at you and they can see your eyes glow

Soon the heart follow
And the thoughts sub side
Wisdom coincides
When the heart get wide

RAMADHAN 20

Rhythm

Celebration starts on the picnic balcony
Green field
High up
Overlooking the Vatican balcony
With a Ka'aba Kube revolving
Somewhere behind your shirt buttons

Your shirt buttons are dotted down you
Like a stripe
Your fingernails are spotted across you
Like a stamp collection
From the bygone age of beauty
You remember, **Before**
When people did not talk nonsense

When words were first being invented
In a posh room
By civilised men with Shakespeare collars, who
Smiled at one another sweetly
Whilst sitting beside elegantly steaming tea
Before a warm English window of countryside

Let's invent a word
One of them thinks

As he remembers the feeling he had
When a woman once touched his arm
In response to a kindness he had rendered her.

His lips begin to give form to the feeling
Framing it with mercy
As it begins to weight
And weight like a raindrop
Becoming more and more pregnant
With each pungent second

Then he says, staring into his colleagues eyes with a smile
"Tennn-der"

His colleague grins widely at this sound
Showing his wonderful yellow teeth
And he instinctively reaches across the table
Placing his hand softly on his friend's wrist
And nodding gently as if to whisper,
'You've done it again'

And they write the word down in their book together.

And the book has pages
One after the other

Regular

Like the stripes and stamps
On us

And the inner contours
In us

Which bend together like a male and female in ballet
Looking out romantically
To a sun and moon
To blades of grass
Or Stars

Big-Sanity is punctuated everywhere
In thorough patterns
All across the sign-posted
Whirling world

RAMADHAN 22
A HIP-HOP VERSE

No-one in America knows what is a "Fiver"
I take my time like a taxi driver
Nod my head when I feel alive, I
Don't know the line, when/know I should stop
I push the boundaries hard that's why I'm obscure
I'm sure, people don't know what to think and that's pure

Don't want no fame or no function, just true reaction
Let me study your face when you see me in action
Let's talk about tangential things with real passion
See the creases in your trousers give ample ammunition
For people like Aldous Huxley and me to feel happy

I love when people say cliche's, it makes me happy
I love when people get in a lift (or elevator)
And look down at the floor and softly wish that it was
Seconds later
I love it when you say goodbye and there's moments it's
akward
Why is it akward?
It's 'cos love wants to expand

Love never really wants to go home all alone.
Love is the primary spring from which you drip
When you drip little drips of your human-self
Which peel like a novel in little ways you can't help
Drip like little poems you write for your health
Drip like little poems that you write for your health....

Over pages over ages over moments in time
Over pages over ages over moments in time
Over pages over ages over moments in time

RAMADHAN 23
ONLY TO BE WITH YOU AND NO-ONE ELSE
For David Miliband & Hilary Clinton

As for an *iftar*[6]
I prefer a quiet one
Without the presence of any bloody bridge builders
Shmoozers or politicians.
If you want to build bridges, go to war zones
And bring plenty of cement.
Don't come to the Mosque smiling in your suit
With a gang of photographers and
Second-rate reporters who will
Write the whole thing up
Just to prove that it happened and
Tick it off a check-list.

Islam is unique to each country it goes to.
In Senegal, they play music more
In Mali, they make mosques out of mud
In Chechnya, strong, bearded men do soft, Sufi dances
And in the West, iftars are social networking opportunities
Never-ending buffets
Part of government strategies to reach out to the
Izlahmic world

But I do not want to be *Af-Pak*'d
Or healed
I do not want to join you on the acceptable side
Where every insecure fool thinks they know
Exactly what extremism is

Nor do I want to laugh and socialise with you at this

---

[6] The breaking of the fast at sunset, traditionally a simple glass of water or milk, with an odd number (usually one or three) dates.

56

Small and
Tender time.

I wish to be alone
And serious
And deeper in love
With the only one who ever matters

the dream

Ramadhan 24

Black Pepper

Pepper *must* fears no dragon or mustard garlic masters of
fortune and war who do not corroborate their plans with
moral backbones are bound to backbite and bite too often on
thunder satisfaction like wild dogs under the full moon of
medieval Europe where the raggedy suripanta woman dances
far too well for a draconian taste of stiffened upper lips and
neck ties and collars and suspenders and wall street and
protestors and newscasters and justice-mongers of the left
and dancers of the right who talk into the night and at dawn
secretly laugh to a god they do not believe in for fear of a
border control of the soul and an end to the American desire
dream of cup-cakes and ice and everything tight

White Salt

Give bread to the mothers and caretakers of your blud-hearts
who save up all their days to see a single sunbirth upon your
face of rhythm of marriage and of child, again as before it
was.

Smiling faces
Good intentions

Place your trust
In someone

The larger the
One
The larger the
Sun

RAMADHAN 26

The cry of the struggler is silenced
It is never heard or acknowledged
It goes into the night
Like time
Droops down and away
Like moon

Like good-bye-moon

The stand of the defiant is statue
Events cannot change
What it has destiny-decided
No human can call it away
From it's steel foundation

Eternal foundation

It is somewhere in between that we mostly reside.

Our generation is inconsistent.
Doesn't know whether to laugh or cry, and can do both
within seconds of each other.

We love some pity, even when we have not earned it and
Do not deserve it, we will accept and
Welcome it.

It is hard not to eat at least one Baklava when your
Emirati host sits a whole plate of them before you.

And there are sweets everywhere
Blinking and ringing down the decorated streets
Where Allah's theatre is dedicated to offering

Beauty, bounty, bribery
Tests.

The clouds are purple and overcast
Upon enchanted hearts that have
Magic and infinity
Running out of them.

.God breathed softly
Into our bodies.

So make me Mansur Al-Hallaj
And heal me with any punishment you wish
Any judgments you can think of

For I have seen now and truly know
That He abounds in me
And that I am a broken piece
A rusty screw
That once was a part of
A ~~beautiful~~ new-tiful view

The original Palace
Where beyond belongs
Where stars are started
And majesty minted.

Whatever I make a defiant stand on these days, whatever
issue I become a firm and moral statue for, and however
strong a spine I stay in the face of sin-suggestion

My foundation
My Palaces and Fortresses

Will always be of clouds
And mist

Echoes

of the original
Voice

From the original
Breath

Ramadhan 29
Freestyle Short Story Written in Under Ten Minutes

So easy to soar. He is in a flight of the year gone and past. His eyes are dissolved from the lids and nothing but the patterns and sun-memories glide before him, nothing but the visions of his imagination cruise through and around him. What a trip.

The ocean, it hurts to have known its power. It hurts to have been robbed and destroyed by it. But isn't dissolution the whole show? We do not apologize to the friend we have wronged because we do not want to sting our pride and humiliate ourselves. But isn't humiliation the only way? Who learned anything from cheerfulness anyway? Anyway?

Oh, these questions and more ran through the little hair's mind all of it's life. It was a white hair, the third white hair on her head. She had seen them come at 24, and it never sunk in that they were really white hairs. She saw them, but she couldn't accept the reality of the situation, she could not so quickly adjust herself to the fact that she was one of those people now, who had white hairs. It is called denial, we all do it, Shakespeare too.

So anyway, this third hair of hers sure has an active imagination. In fact if any scientist were interested enough to study it for the rest of her life, she would eventually find the answers to all of life's questions in this hair. From her human perspective. She'd never know how intelligent the hair was, of course. This would remain hidden to her.

The hair did not have a name, so I won't give it one. I'm a human being, talking the language of humans, so forgive me if I have to resort to calling it 'the third hair'.

This third hair was called Meshell. Me, Shell. She stole this name from a shell, when once upon a time the head she belonged to lay down on a beach one day in England. Of all places, why lie down in an English beach, thought the third hair. Question mark. But lie down she did (the woman whose head it was). Her name was Aisha and she was not Arab or Pakistani, so take that, two thirds of the people who will be reading this! If you want to empathize with the character, I am not going to give you any easy rides. We're going to have to go for the heart this time, guys. Looks like we're going to have to bypass the material matter and go straight for the soul to find our commonality, guys. Team. Friends. Lovers. Hearties.

When Aisha put her head down onto the pebbles, third hair was lucky enough to not be face down. Third hair was lucky enough to be sideways, and she was looking out at a shell which lay right next to her. She said to the Shell, (all things are in constant communication with one another, including your eyes and my intentions)

"What's your name, then?"
"Me, Shell,"

Said the shell.

Nice name, thought third hair…

That clears that up.

Now let's get onto the good stuff. The juicy part. About the human called Aisha who is not from Arabistan or Pakistan. Shall we make her fall in love? No! No! Why? Why would we want to do such a boring thing with her? She has so much going for her already! She has her third white hair talking to sea-shells, and plenty of other things besides.

Aisha shimmers under the glimmering sun which shivers her anew into this world like a baby again. She had never thought that possible, never thought optimistically enough to think that a moment such as this would come, a moment with light and strong bells that softly were touched by angels-of-the-moment and made her rise and rise and rise to never fall for those moments where everything seemed balanced on serenity and clarity, happiness and precision. What more is there to aim for but these moments?

Her fingers moved one by one as Muslim fingers do, and the Names were repeated in her head one by one, as Muslim minds do. With gratitude and chants, such as the people of sincerity do all across this bouncy ball.

It is not trendy is it? No longer trendy to talk of God and of the *word*, even, to make such people cringe and want to leave the vicinity. No it is not. And yet there she lay, with the afternoon sun of September, hot but not killing, hot but welcome, and the breeze on her nose, and all of the parts of her body which worked in harmony to continue her

Agreeing absolutely.

Her nose agreeing with the scent of freshness. Her ears with the sound of the distant couple. Her eyes with the blue above and her mind with the abode. Her mind with the throne from which all legacies and histories unfold.

Never enough illustriousness in this day and age. Never enough perfection and unbounded parting emotion for hearts

to die in and cry in love for separation and union and please
and please, please, God, please.

The headline on CNN.com reads:

Rape claim 'traumatizing,' former suspect says

Inner the heart of health there is no headline, no loud sign or
large fonts. Only a rushing of rising, of falling, floating
pantheons and disembodied Greek pillars revolving upside
down and going with all seriousness into the moon's open
arms where it spills to dust

To dust

Dust.

Ramadhan 30
EID OFFERING

Gold

God

Amber

Angel

Resin

Relative

Raisin

Reflective

Paramount

Majesty

Marvelous

Momentum

Purple

Still

Still

Still

The Beautiful (Recontinued)

RETURNING DREAM ABOUT ETERNITY
(A HIP-HOP VERSE)

Black star
Bathing in Black Moonlight
Body Blue Gold
Give a Grand for Breast Milk

Milk the Million, Man
The Civilised
Trillion Heart
Start the Maximillion

You wriggling baby
Stuck on a Black Moon
Dark half cast on your
Saviours' eyes, soon

Come, the White Crack in the
Velveteen, seen
Scratch in the Black of the Starry Screen

With One God
One Text in the Fire-y dreams
The Fire-Flame[s] Fly
And they fan to Free Man

Shapes in the Wood
And the Clouds and Smoke
Ijtihad,[7] my main Guard is the Symbol
I walk this _____ Earth with a shield of
Abstract thoughts and a
Belief in Beauty

---

[7] Islamic concept of using ones own personal interpretation

Dreams they go by every day when I wake up
And put on my shoes and my masculine make-up

Ego slick and my earthly energy
Ain't got no thing on my Chastified Dark Nights
Ain't got a thing on my Sanctified Searchers
My Jesus, Muhammad and my Moses Cursors.

Black Blood in my Body is Billion
Built for All-Time and my Frame is Freedom
Five Fingers Move just so you can See dem
Eyes spill Soul, you don't need to read 'em
Your Body is a-Rocking to the Rhythm of Eden
Don't think where just Put the Black Seed in
You and me both, from a Spark of Semen.

For / by Ishmael Butler, again

Brandished polished pushers
Hexagram gram grammarian man
Motion marvel at the mansion Mercutio
Build and Guild, the Gilded crest waves of next
Flex spine-water-wisdom when it
Curves to freedom
Curving to freedominion dome-dome-delight
Full far away sands see the star-tipped turqoise
Crescent in the eye-sky
Grandio-galax.
Go for green-gallons of the
Ocean, sip down.

GIVING (HANDSOMELY)

At night
I sit by a computer
With a brilliant blue shawl draped around me
And over my head

Seated
I shoot off sparks to the ends of the Earth
24 thousand miles of
Running
        Care

  Streamers
    of
  Water
   and
  Kindness

To keep this world spinning on
Someone's amazement at just
How can a stranger be this nice
To me who he's never met?

To keep it unfolding with love for when I'm gone
As the others like me do
Undertaking tasks far too nice as to be realistic
And to inspire in the hearts of the seedlings
An infinity of openings for
What it is possible to do and be
On this planet

THE SPANGLE MAKER

Dear God
You have unleashed me again.
Turned me out onto the streets again.
Made me leave a budding love again.
Made me wander homeless again.

I love you more than I am able to love.

I reach out to hold you as I hold clouds that surround me and
Hug you as I do dreams which are
Real but un-huggable by arms.

I drink you as I think you
I steel you as I feel you
Reach you as I speak you

BLUSTERY

We look at each other with such desire
Everybody wants someone so badly
But nobody wants anyone more than they want themselves

◘

Seek out coffee like money
Run for it

◘

I've tasted satisfaction
It made me sick

◘

Make the proud ones happy
Tell them they're *great*
(It feels nice, remember?)

◘

I love tender little adult men with small bodies and big heads
who don't have enough of a stake in anything to be
disappointed and who would never get angry. Such people
never encroach too far onto any territory; they take baby
steps everywhere and have the aura of a young man who is
just happy to have been invited to the party. That's why they
smile and go about either shy or wide-eyed (depending on
how much citrus God put into their souls).

It's true that they might not marry, might die alone. But if
they do marry, what a daily beacon they would become for
the uninspired streets and offices they breeze through!

You may be a rocket alone, but marriage makes you a nebula.

SUNSETS

The birds leave
Binding another sunset
Bonded in bleeding belief and
Besmoothing saline balm of
Explosion

Close to closing time
Everyone stops being so friendly
And wants you
                    Out

The dark blue lume
Streets are coming alive

Beauty has nowhere to go
But through every layer
Piercing

Cry or don't

BLACK FUTURE

God,
When you make me an olden
Man,
Will I be resigned to things like the rest of them?

That is what I fear most,
  Oh Lord.

Will I be sighing and waving ideas away with a weak wrinkly
Hand, which knows it has
No strength to stop a bullet
Or make a fist
Or resist a nurses spoon
Of moist, liquidized chicken?

Is that resignation all due to the failure of ones knees which
Betray like friends you thought you could rely on, who
walked out on you and took your car keys with them?

If that's all it is
I can stand it
Or sit it
I can make my mind stronger
…Counterbalance, etc.

What I fear, oh Creator of Eternity
Is that it's a losing battle no matter what.
I fear it not getting more beautiful
And closing up on me like a flower in October
at Seven o clock
                    No matter how much fuel I put in
                              For the rainy day

OLD MOONS

Old moons now are dried and crusty
Brittle and as uninteresting as history is
To my fingers and lips.

And yet also, it cannot be denied
That each man
King of his home-throne
Misses something of eternity
When he chomps down on lamb chops
(Which are his reward
For winning the bread)

Each of us misplace the universe
And lose the word
When we get our desires
On plates before us.

There is a grain of rice on the table.
Around it, oil has bled
And spreads

In this way does our egodeath
Halo around us
  And puncture the beauty
    Of clouds

ALWAYS FALL / SAD END

When you're in a building like this,
the idea of butterflies seems quite ridiculous.

Of course the ceilings are high.
Of course there are drops of water falling from certain areas.
Or course it's entirely abandoned and emptied.

Not because it's old though. Oh no. That would be a mistake,
if you are picturing an old building. No, to me, looking from
the stairwell, it seems like a perfectly modern building. The
only problem seems to be that it's empty. And that some of
the lights are flickering on and off. And every now and then
you step into a little puddle.

But that doesn't matter, because you're wearing hard black
boots. Aren't you ? AREN'T YOU???

You're covered from head to toe in hard things which, which
don't let the world in.

And as you walk up these stairs, there's a mission, a cold
mission on your mind. Your brain has been frozen and tuned
to the frequency of that mission. So that nothing else enters
your thoughts. No memories. No children tugging at your
trouser legs, no white English butterflies, no black American
ones either. No dogs, no kisses, no white bed-sheets, no
morning-suns, no blue skies, no morning-walks, no
newspapers and thoughts of smiling famous people who you
love or hate.

No voices in the room next door, also painted white or cream.

You have a pin-sphered mind like a spider angling your way

to the target, walking at a steady pace up the stairwell. Such steadiness is for robots and spiders and deadly men. Men who don't talk. And your mouth is always closed as you march.

You're nearing the top of it now. You stupid bastard soldier, you. You bloody fool. You're almost there. Accomplishment.

You open the final door with your slow and powerful wrists. You twist it nice and calmly. You're in the penthouse of the world trade center on the night of September 11th. You're still high up in the sky because it never fell down. You're on the 107th floor. There's a little plane sticking out of your chest, but other than that, you're okay.

You push the door open and what's inside? What's inside this little dark room? You flick the switch but it doesn't work. That's okay. You soldiers always come prepared, you're prepared for everything, like Batman. You take out a lighter and chick it. *Chick, CHICK CHICK.* The third chick reveals something quite strange, but not altogether unexpected. There's a little blonde girl sitting at the end of the room. From the small reflection of the lighter you can make out that she's around 15 years old, and wearing red-lipstick. Her eyes are wide open, staring out at the huge window. You go right up behind her, towards her ear, and you whisper, "What's happening here sister?"

She turns to fully face you, her eyes near your lips. She smiles like Kim Basinger and says, "I'm not your sister! Which means!" Then she grabs your hand and pulls you towards the door. One tug, then two. Three is all it takes for the soldier to forget his stupid mission. A pretty young woman is all it needs. She runs, with your hand and lagging body behind her. You're probably smiling stupidly as she takes you out of the room. Then suddenly you see the glass windows all around you. And the lights of the city are calling you. And so you run, all the way down to the end of the corridor! And the faster you run together, the more she looks at you and says, "YES! **YES!!!** LETS <u>**DO IT!**</u>" You are getting closer to the window, and you decide, what the hell? That is your decision.

You jump headfirst into the glass and worry that it's not going to brake. But it does. It shatters with the magnificence worthy of such a strong man. You smile as the high air hits you in the face. You turn to your right to see the pretty young girl, her creamy teeth smiling from inside the red red lipstick. But she's not there. She's not there smiling with you. You look back upwards, to the window you smashed and are now falling from. She's standing inside it, waving sadly to you. She seems to be saying, 'I'd like to, I really would, but I'm just too young. I've got too much ahead of me. Good luck though!'

Stupid little girl is talking as if she doesn't know what you've sacrificed.

And down you rustle with the wind and your normal clothes. You wear a lumberjack's shirt now, and loose khaki trousers. The wind makes them feel good. You open your mouth wide for the first time and out comes a butterfly. Meaning that you will definitely die alone. But at least you had fun...

NO MYSTERY #2

Perhaps I will never again
As much as I, and we
Did for those years
Of discovery

And if I don't
Ever again
As much as we did
I don't know what I will do
I don't know what will become of me

In nearly all things
One can learn patience and moderation

One can work the career ladder
As the days turn to months and
Paychecks blend into some
Warbling, unknown quantity of meaningless
Money.
One will always have a foresighted approach if serious
About some 'thing'
Always wait with the eye on the prize
Patience is very easy with finance and career

But not with *that*

The body is not made to burn everlasting
And I cannot stand to think of
Losing you
(Another like you
Who would make me feel as
You did)
When once my body has

Begun to dry
As it has been
All of these tiring years, post-you

Post-our
      Starship sailings
            Down the Niles of
                  Our happy hearts
                      Yearning for one another
                As we row and row
          Sweat and grow inside
      Towards one another's core
Where we

Saw

What we loved

Without it I'll die forever
Without it I won't be free forever

Wherever and whoever you are
Whatever form you take
From whichever crater you arise
And with whatever darkness you bring

              Come!

              Find me out

And *soon*

Make it *soon!*

Afterwords

This is an afterword to my new poetry book by me the one who wrote it. I am writing it because I could not be bothered to ask anybody else to do so; also because I wanted the opportunity to write about something which is presently far enough removed by time so as not to cause me convulsions and tears.

In early June of 2009, I was visiting family in North Carolina, in a very small beach-town called Surf City. Someone I have known all my life swam very far out to the sea and I suddenly was overcome by fear that this person had swam too far and was going to be in trouble. I thought she was going to die. I swam furiously out. I lied when I said this subject would be easy to write about because it is already forcing me to take deep breaths in as I write. I cannot write about it.

Let me simply say this, without an in-depth description. I found myself astray, I almost drowned completely and I almost was not here. I was close to death. I can say that. I faced it almost fully; maybe completely fully. I, I, I. Death. It is too big to talk about.

I have not known, in the six months since then, what to make of it. I met and spoke with Shaykh Hisham Kabbani of the Naqshbandi Sufi order when he came to visit Virginia a month or so after the event. He was kind. I also read a lot about death. Perhaps none of these books were very helpful because none of them were new. I have always thought a great deal about my own death. My favorite films, the ones which make me cry most, have always been about life and its ending (Weir's *Fearless*, Kore-Eda's *Maboroshi*, Lynch's *Elephant Man* and Huston's masterful rendition of *Night of the*

Iguana, to name but four of many). I have dreamt of it through the years, and pondered it very often. Needless to say, when I was out there, very far out in the ocean, and realizing that this was truly 'it,' the irony of it hit me. Before the final moments of desperation, there was a small little unimportant voice in my head, the sort of voice that makes 'points' and he was trying to raise the point of how ironic this was, that I was now facing that very thing which I had so often, on train rides and in parks, and in every other random place imaginable, thought about at my own leisure. He then made the point of how ridiculous this situation was, how just ten minutes before I had arrived at the beach, on holiday, and now I was so very far out and the seriousness of my thoughts had suddenly deepened a million times. Then that little voice tried to whisper what had happened to a man called Cat Stevens, and how this was almost too ironic in it's similarity to his accident, given that my name is also Yusuf. But the larger thoughts soon took over and drowned out that little voice. They had to. Indeed, the last conscious / mundane thought I had was to tell that little voice to shut up, because this was serious, this was not a joke I was in.

The larger thoughts were saying, "Is this it? Can this really be it? What will happen without me? What will all the people I know think of this? Of the fact that I had drowned."

It was all so horrible to think about. Those thoughts rushed me. And soon, even those thoughts would be rendered mundane. The sea was so large that it makes me very shaky to think about it now. I don't remember seeing anything so huge in my life, but when you consider that you are in the middle of it, and it is all around you- again, I am not good enough with words to describe how very scary it is, how very puny and nothing it makes you feel. People say this sort of thing all the time, and their words, as mine, are useless. But I would not wish the feeling on anyone. It is fear of enormity. A primal fear one can only feel in the face of huge-ness. Limitlessness.

When my strength had almost been sapped entirely, and my body was beginning to give in, and the desperate gulps for air began turning into gulps of sickly-tasting ocean-water because my neck was too exhausted to lift my head up... That is the precise moment that I prayed. I literally had nothing left, no thoughts, and now, no energy. I had accepted that I was without a hope but one, which had somehow not come to me except at that final moment. What was my prayer? And why would I be sharing it with you? I have no idea regarding the latter question.

My prayer was:

"I'll do better. I'll be better." [If you save me].

I did not verbalise (in my mind) the desire to be saved, but such a thing is implied in that situation, and/or perhaps I was saving my energy, for even thoughts –at that moment– even thoughts were taking up energy in my head, which felt empty and beyond-dizzy, and now heavy, and which the hard-hard sun beat down upon angrily.

I cannot put it another way but this: moments after I said the prayer, I began to feel one last reserve of energy which had come from nowhere. It came organically, it was real, and I was suddenly aware of a new capacity that I could tap into. And I said consciously to myself, 'this is your last chance.' I took two strong strokes with my arms, despite the fact that my shoulders had officially died many minutes before. Those two strokes were the only ones I took, and then I felt myself being pushed back to the distant shore (all of this time, the people were the size of slightly larger ants, lined up at the shore, staring at me as I tried to scream for help). The relentless "rip-tide" I was caught in began to release me. Slowly. And what seemed like moments later, perhaps minutes, I felt the slightest of slightest (yet undeniable, discernible) brushes of sand on the very end of one of my toes. And slowly, painfully slowly, with only the now-friendly tide half-enthusiastically pushing my finished body forwards, I was pushed back onto the safe sands of people. Fat, tanning people. Cowardly, too scared to have come after me when I screamed, people. Kind and now so caring people. Beautiful, such beautiful people.

I've spent the last six months incredibly scared and also incredibly upset at my inability to effect a dramatic change in my life for the better. I am not one for big dramatic things, perhaps. But this, surely, called for a dramatic change. Subtlety is something I have always, probably in a self-righteous way, made it a point to emphasize, to live in, it has become second nature to me. But after the tremendous sense of destiny and fortune that one feels after being rescued from what is, literally, a desperate situation (and you will not know what desperate means until you've felt death that close, until you have come as close as I had to accepting that you are about to die) then it is difficult to put into words just how disappointed you can feel with yourself if, in the immediate aftermath, you do not see large strokes, huge dramatic and active improvements, actions towards improvements, even. It is difficult to put across how guilty one feels for lazing around or killing time, and yet still doing those things because of bad habits. After such an overwhelming gratitude, to have been saved just by a brush of a wave, a turn, a mercy, which had nothing to do with your powerless self.

In being *better*, which was my promise, I can, if I grasp hard, only say that I have perhaps entered a productive stage whereby my ever increasing back-log of creative works is being slightly eased by the imminent release of my new album, my second novel, and perhaps this short book eventually too. But that is nothing to feel happy about. It was spiritual depth and improvement that my prayer referred to. Nothing but that. When I was drowning, between the end of my struggling and just before my prayer, I remember feeling that every single thing I had done in my life had been a waste, creativity included. Poetry included. I felt that, and relay it now, in complete truth. I had not concerned myself with Him, and He it was who was talking to me now, and He it was who mattered. Nobody else; no *thing* else. The subject? Being closer to Him. I don't know that I'll ever find such a proximity with the Unseen Force, with God, for as long as I am alive. Not as much as I had in those few moments. It was just me and the ocean. We were alone, creator to creation. I made a deal. If I ever do feel such proximity again I should hope it comes under different circumstances, at moments where I may enJOY it. Fear and trembling, as Kierkegaard had it, are one essential part of faith. Love, Joy and Ecstasy are the other. This incident made me respect and revere that Fear which I had never quite understood. It made me respect true, elemental, divine Power and it made me comprehend what powerlessness and dependence really mean. I use the feelings I had in those moments every single day now.

The poems from 'The Automatic Sky' onwards were all written after this accident (which incidentally, I am still paying ridiculously large hospital/ambulance bills for, so thank you for your support). I suppose I wanted you to know all of this. That is why I am writing it for you. We are, after all, a team. We are, after all, twinned at the heart, part of the same source. I do, after all, regard you as me, and my closest human *possibles*. It was for you that I wondered, in a general way, as I struggled so desperately, 'what will they think?' I do not speak of my audience, for as I know best, I have but a small handful of kind lovers whom I might credibly call an audience, but rather of *potentials*, potential partners, friends and helpers and receivers in this life. This very short life.

And this week, I look toward another journey for the spirit (this time a visit to Cyprus, which I am making because of a particularly vivid dream I had of a man some two weeks ago) where I hope I might find something of what it is that I need. Some beginning route towards 'better-ness,' that I may live with and embark upon. There's scant motivation in the abstract notion of merely fulfilling a promise, a *deal*. And so that is not truly why I go. I wish to be better because *I wish to be better*. The accident was a cruel but needed reminder of what I have always known, but too easily put off: that we must move constantly in a motion towards perfection. Not be satisfied to stay still. And to this end, if this artist can ever be close to even a beginning of True Satisfaction, then it might mean an end to his art, and this could well be my last book of poetry, my last creative work! If that be the cost for a road to true and deep spiritual fulfillment, then I should be glad to say goodbye to the closest friend that I have had on Earth. I should be more than willing to put an end to this beautifully insane journey of love and art which began in the very early parts of this decade. Because this life is too short to make excuses on behalf of your material ambitions; too short for unhappiness; too short for putting up with too much sadness today with only a faint and vague hope of liberation ahead. The means must be as crystal clear to us as the ends. And they must feel right as we undertake them.

Peace and love,
Yusuf Misdaq
Washington DC, December 27th, 2009.

Reciting 'The Beautiful' at Subcontinental Drift, Washington DC, Summer 2009

Also available & coming soon from Yusuf Misdaq

Lefke Automatic / Destiny of Love (Poetry)	NEFI-BK07
The Butterfly Gate (Poetry)	NEFI-BK05
Spilling Kingdoms (Poetry)	NEFI-BK04
Into Solidity (Poetry)	NEFI-BK03
Brighton Streets (Poetry)	NEFI-BK02
Pieces of a Paki (Novel)	NEFI-BK01
[No Title] (Documentary)	NEFI-CD03
Maghreb, Isha & Space (Music, LP)	NEFI-CD03
Flowers & Trees (Music, LP)	NEFI-CD02
From a Western Box (Music, LP)	NEFI-CD01

Narayan (Novel)
The Steep Ascent (Novel)

CPSIA information can be obtained at www.ICGtesting.com
Printed in the USA
269995BV00001B/1/P